Humble

&

The Robin & The Sparrow

(Illustrated)

By
Charlie Forrestt

Copyright© 2020 Charlie Forrestt

Written by Charlie Forrestt

Cover Design by Charlie Forrestt

Cover artwork and illustrations by Dan Digby (https://www.facebook.com/DigbyComics) (https://www.instagram.com/drd_comic_artist)

Disclaimer: This is a work of fiction. All of the characters, places and events portrayed in this novel are either products of the author's imagination or are used fictitiously.

Published by
The Alderbourne Press Ltd

First edition 2013
Second edition 2014
Third Edition 2018
Fourth Edition 2020

Table of Contents

Author's Note

'Humblenot and The Robin & The Sparrow' is a story written by Charlie Forrestt for children of all ages. This story introduces the character, 'Humblenot', a storyteller, a forest dweller, a human-like creature who may once have been a brave crusading Knight, but he might also have been a dragon handler.

Today, Humblenot is telling the story of 'The Robin and The Sparrow' and what happened when Robin flew in from the south for the winter to find Sparrow had been left behind. Being the first Humblenot story, you are introduced to some of the other characters who live in the village: the Constable and the Schoolmistress feature in this story.

The story you are about to read is really three stories in one. We will learn something of Humblenot, who he is and where he lives but more importantly perhaps, of what he does. Within these pages, we join the children of the village as they all gather around Humblenot to listen while he tells the tale of 'The Robin and The Sparrow'; a story where Robin will tell his own tale to Sparrow; the one that explains how all robins came to have red breasts.

Each Humblenot story will reveal more about him and the place where he lives but he will always tell a story. However, his stories won't always be just for the children because as you will see, grown-ups like to hear his stories too!

'Humblenot and The Robin & The Sparrow' is published for Kindle and is available exclusively in the Amazon Kindle Store. The story is also published as a paperback and again, available exclusively through Amazon.

Best Wishes,

Charlie Forrestt

Contact Us!

Our website address is:
https://thealderbournepress.com/

Charlie Forrestt

CHAPTER ONE

The twins, Yannick and Annick, who, strictly speaking, should have been in the schoolroom, were in the orchard. Their excuse for being in the orchard and not in the schoolroom was pretty thin. Old Mother Eve had asked them why and the answer, delivered by Annick, was either fact or fiction and as indistinguishable as the twins themselves.

"Mother Eve; Farmer Orin has asked us to count the good apples in the orchard."

"Why did Farmer Orin ask you to count the good apples in the orchard?"

"Farmer Orin impressed upon us the importance of ascertaining, within a margin of error consistent with the square root of *Pi*, the number of good apples versus the number of bad as an indication of the prospects of filling the Duchess' cider barrels."

Not entirely convinced that the boys were telling the truth, Old Mother Eve popped in and spoke to the Constable.

"Thank you for telling me, Mother Eve. I shall make investigations this very afternoon and if the twins were trying, as we know they do, to avoid algebra - and goodness knows we all did in our time - then I shall speak to the twins and remind them that no good can come of this. The present and the future must always be balanced like the equation they so assiduously avoid. But there is no avoiding it!"

"Thank you, Constable. Oh! Humblenot is back."

"HUMBLENOT!"

"Yes, Constable. He is back!"

The Constable, who had been enjoying his lunch of bread, cheese, and pickled gherkins, was suddenly not very hungry and felt the prickling in his chest, which was the precursor to indigestion.

"Humblenot ... is my job not hard enough without you stirring up the village with your tales of faraway places?"

Reaching for the camomile tea, he did have to reflect just briefly on the tales that Humblenot had told him when he had been the same age as the twins; tales of princes fighting wars and leading their armies on the backs of elephants. Stories that were like wormholes leading to strange, imaginary kingdoms ruled by ants and where algebra was confined to the palace dungeons.

Though his job required him to be stern and serious, he could not prevent himself from smiling, just for a minute, at the prospect of hearing another of Humblenot's stories.

By the time he had walked to the orchard, the twins were nowhere to be found. He marched purposefully to the farm and found Farmer Orin milking the cow.

"Did you ask the twins to count the good apples in the orchard, Farmer Orin?"

"Well, I do remember being asked by the twins if there was something they could do that was more important than balancing quadratic equations."

"Nothing is more important than balancing quadratic equations, Farmer!"

"I disagree. Filling the Duchess' cider barrels is infinitely more important than balancing quadratic equations."

"I do not believe that the Duchess would sanction the removal of two children from the schoolroom for the express purpose of filling her cider barrels."

"Constable; you would do well to remember that the Duchess likes cider more than she likes children!"

"The children's education must be our first priority. They are the future."

"I believe that, in giving the twins this task and insisting upon a thorough report of the condition of the apples, I have served their education just as well as Mistress Jane would have done in the schoolroom this morning."

"Maybe you did, but they missed French grammar too!"

"I do not think that either Yannick or Annick are destined to become an Ambassador, Constable."

"We deny them the choice by colluding in this mischief."

"Humblenot is back."

"I KNOW! My indigestion is as good a barometer as that which hangs outside the forge! Good day, Farmer."

"Good day, Constable."

The Farmer Orin returned to milking the cow and paid no attention to the rustling and giggling he heard coming from the hayloft.

The Constable was a burly man and afraid of nothing. Well, that wasn't strictly true. He was afraid of the Duchess and the corner of the forest inhabited by Humblenot. And if you pressed him on the point, he was more afraid of the Duchess than the forest, especially if the cider barrels were half-full come Festival time.

"I suppose I must call upon him. It is one o'clock and there is plenty of time to get to the forest and back before sunset," he counselled himself as he straightened his tunic and polished the toecaps of his boots on the backs of his trouser legs.

Striding through the village, he passed the church and the schoolroom. Silence from the schoolroom indicated that French grammar was in full swing.

He avoided the forge in case he got soot on his uniform.

The post office was closed being a Wednesday afternoon, but he tried the door in any case. Abigail the Postmistress often forgot to lock the door, and when she did, the stamps used the opportunity to send themselves to interesting and faraway places.

He made his way along the path that led to the Magistrate's house. The Magistrate was in session; the long-running dispute between Angela the Seamstress and Rosemary the Hat Maker was being heard for the seventeenth time. The argument over who owned the fence between their gardens had been running ever since the Constable had taken up his position.

Conscious of the time, he quickened his steps and took the shortcut across the Festival Field.

He climbed over the stile and met the Postmistress in the lane.

"Good afternoon, Postmistress."

"Good afternoon, Constable. Do I assume from your direction of travel that you are paying Humblenot a visit?"

"You are correct in your assumption."

"If you are quick you might get there before the story starts."

"To whom is he telling stories at this time of the day?"

"The children."

"Ah! That is why the schoolroom was silent. I supposed French grammar to be the cause."

"I understand that Mistress Jane is keen to introduce the children to the art of storytelling and no-one tells a story as well as Humblenot."

"It is true. Do you remember his tale of the Persian Prince and the magic-?"

The Constable cut himself off abruptly.

"I do. We were all nine years old once, Constable. A fact we would be wise to remind ourselves of from time to time. Enjoy the story ..."

The Constable said goodbye and continued on his way. Very soon he was under the boughs of the young oaks where the path was well-made and quite dry. The Constable and mud did not have a happy relationship!

Deeper into the forest he went, and the air surrounding him was thick with the hum of bees.

If the Farmer Orin was working hard to fill the cider barrels, the bees were working even harder to fill the hives with honey!

The path wound around the Major; an oak of majestic proportions which was believed to be older than the Duchess.

Legend had it that Humblenot had planted the oak; a fact that he would neither confirm nor deny.

Whether he had buried the heart of a lion under the oak was pure speculation.

The Constable skirted around the edge of the gravel pit and along the stream bed until he came to the abandoned watermill.

He dipped his cupped hand into the stone trough that sat outside the door of the mill and brought a mouthful of sweet spring water to his lips.

As expected, the waterwheel unexpectedly started to turn. The creak of the timbers made him shiver and the helmet on his head wobbled like a jelly.

"Nail your courage to the sticking place, Augustus!" he said to himself.

He continued on his way, reminding himself that if the children had walked to Humblenot's house then he, a burly constable, must surely not allow himself to be any more afraid than they had been.

Recalling himself as a nine-year-old walking through the forest and holding fast onto Henrietta's hand, made him feel better. Until he remembered the day she had let go of his hand at the Witches' Willow. He had been so afraid that he had stayed the whole night, shaking like a leaf and curled up into a tight ball like a hedgehog. Humblenot had rescued him and carried him back to the village.

The Witches' Willow was ahead, and beads of perspiration broke out on his forehead and his hands felt cold and clammy.

Old Mother Eve always said that if you passed the Witches' Willow on your left it was better than if you passed it on your right. In addition, you should always appear to be looking for acorns and whistle the Duchess' Birthday Song.

He passed with the tree on his left and scanned the ground for acorns. The dry tuneless whistle that passed between his pursed lips was echoed by the rustle of the leaves.

Having passed the tree safely, he climbed the giant molehill and, once out of sight of the Witches' Willow, gave thanks to the composer of the tune for his safe deliverance. The composer of the tune, albeit grateful for the thanks, would have preferred a penny in royalties!

The last stage of the path was by far the most terrifying. The trees were truly ancient. The trunks and branches had grown into a living palace, not that Humblenot called it such. The bark of the trees looked like the skins of snakes and lizards and many were covered in warts like the Hammer Pond toads.

Thin creepers hung down to form curtains that hid dark and dank places where oozy and slimy things lived. If you were brave enough, or foolhardy enough, to part the creepers and look behind them, you would see vats of green gunge being boiled to make ink or cough mixture, depending upon the season.

Passing through the space between the two trees that looked like dragons, the Constable arrived at the home of Humblenot.

Fifty feet in front of him was the toadstool garden, and upon each toadstool sat a child, like a pixie. All the boys wore moss green shorts and mustard coloured shirts, Raven black-blue socks and chestnut brown leather boots, while all the girls wore strawberry red dresses, lilac stockings, and wooden clogs.

The Schoolmistress was dressed in grey as befitted her advanced years and station. Her hair, these days grey, was held up in a bun. Two sparrows, one with a smart red jacket, had nested in it but no-one had seen fit to mention it.

The toadstool garden sat in front of Humblenot's house if indeed 'house' could be used to describe his abode. It was certainly not like any other house but then there was no-one quite like Humblenot.

CHAPTER TWO

Humblenot was not sitting in the storytelling chair and at that precise moment, he was nowhere to be seen. He must have been expected very soon because all of the children were holding their breath. The Constable caught the eye of the Schoolmistress and nodded very stiffly. The Schoolmistress inclined her head in return.

A sound like granite being put through the sausage maker could be heard but where the noise was coming from, no-one could be sure. The Constable advanced a little and noticed that the twins were seated on the toadstools closest to the storytelling chair.

"Absent for algebra but as keen as the mustard of their shirts to hear the story!" He thought.

How the twins had arrived at the storytelling garden before the Constable could only be guessed at. While he waited for the appearance of Humblenot, the Constable re-acquainted himself with the dwelling in which Humblenot lived when he wasn't travelling to faraway places and collecting stories from gurus and maharajahs.

The closely planted trees behind the chair were the oldest in the forest and their trunks were wider than a man's outstretched arms. Not even an ant could pass between the trunks without having to breathe in. The canopy above the chair was like a vast tent. The interwoven branches and leaves ensured that the ground beneath the canopy remained perfectly dry. The edge of the canopy reached out and covered the toadstool garden. However, the branches were thinner, and the leaves were smaller and therefore sunlight, or moonlight, was able to filter down and illuminate the space. This saved on oil and wicks for the lamps. On dark nights the garden was lit by glow-worms. There was a jar under each toadstool that was home to a glow-worm. Old Mother Eve had the task of feeding the glow-worms and cleaning the jars. In exchange, Humblenot gave her silk thread with which she made stockings for the girls and socks for the boys, which were gifted to them at Christmas time. On Christmas Eve, the socks and the stockings were hung from the mantelpiece in each home, waiting to be filled with a walnut, an orange and a chocolate egg covered in gold foil.

The storytelling chair was positioned at the edge of the garden so that those children, young or old, who were seated at the back, would have no difficulty in hearing the narration. No-one ever complained of not being able to hear the story, not even deaf Jake the Haymaker.

The chair was crafted from ... well, was it stone or wood? It might have once been wood but through age and weathering, the surface resembled carved stone, like the tombs of the Knights in the chapel of the Palace; a chair for a Knight.

The chair had a high back and a deep seat. A chair for a very tall Knight with very long legs!

The Constable's reverie was interrupted by the cessation of the sound of granite being put through a sausage maker, which was then replaced by the tinkle of glasses. Two older children stepped out from the dark recess of the dwelling, carrying a tray of glasses filled with sparkling nettle cordial. Each child took a glass of cordial and gave thanks.

The two older children were the eldest in the village; not yet old enough to start their apprenticeships. The girl, Clara, handed drinks to the younger girls, and the boy, Hugo, handed drinks to the younger boys.

Clara was destined to work for Rosemary the Hat Maker. Hugo was destined to work for Jake the Haymaker. First, they had to pass their final examination.

Clara handed a glass to Mistress Jane and Hugo handed a glass to the Constable. Clara and Hugo took their seats and a blanket of complete hush settled on the garden.

Imagine a thunderstorm that starts small and quiet before it suddenly grows big and loud. This is what the announcement of Humblenot's arrival felt like to those waiting for him. Just as they thought that the thunder could not get any louder or closer, a final clap and a flash of light as bright as a magnesium flare announced the arrival of the renowned storyteller who, by some magic or artifice, was now seated in the chair. He was leaning forward with one arm bent and resting on his leg: his hand supporting his chin. The other arm was stretched out. The hand was extended, and his index finger was pointing at the path that led into the forest.

"Never stray from the path when the moon is hidden ... unless you want an adventure!"

Humblenot's voice was like the river rushing over the cascade; a river swollen by the meltwaters of the spring thaw. In the same roar, you could hear the grinding of rocks tumbling in the rapids. Above the roar and beneath the grinding you might hear, if you concentrated hard enough, the sound of a lark rising or the hoot of an owl. When Humblenot spoke, the air throbbed, the grass quivered, leaves shook, and the dry stems of teasel weeds rattled like the medicine sticks of the Indian Yogis.

All were enrapt from the moment he opened his mouth. In the silence between each sentence, you could hear the footsteps of ants creeping through the garden and the flap of the damsel fly's wings as she fluttered upstream to hide her babies in the lock gate's keyhole.

"Who can tell me where the sparrows go in winter?"

Yannick was first to thrust his hand into the air.

Humblenot inclined his head very slightly and settled his eyes on Yannick, "Speak and permit no falsehood to stain your lips. I see the juice of blackberries on your hands and apple pips between your teeth. Tell me you played truant and spent the morning in the orchard!"

Yannick was a stout boy with the heart of a Bull Dog. Even he shrank into his shirt at the command, though he didn't let his hand fall.

"Humblenot, I would tell you that I aided Farmer Orin today with an important commission. My brother, Annick, and I spent the morning in the orchard counting good apples."

"How many were there?"

"Three thousand, seven hundred and twenty-four."

"One bad apple will spoil a barrel of sixty! Where do the sparrows go for the winter?"

"It if pleases you to know; they fly south and spend the winter on the warm steppes of the equatorial plains."

"It pleases me to hear the right answer."

Humblenot laughed and the toadstools shook, and the children let out a squeal.

"Who wants to hear a story about a sparrow that was left behind?"

"WE DO, HUMBLENOT!" cried the children, and the Constable's voice could be heard above all of the others.

Before Humblenot started the story, he picked up a pail that was sat beside his chair and brought it to his lips. He drank deeply of the contents that smelled of honey and dandelions. As he drank, you could see the liquid flow down his throat and around his innards, curling his toes.

CHAPTER THREE

Humblenot wiped his mouth on the back of his hand and settled himself. He briefly caught the eye of the Constable and licked his lips; like a cat might lick its lips at finding itself in the Palace creamery.

"It was the middle of October and Jack Frost came a-creeping into the forest. He arrived before dawn and caught the dew napping. Not a drop escaped his chilly handshake.

All the creatures of the forest heard the crunch of his steps as he strode back and forth looking for a good place to lay his hearth.

At sunrise, he fell asleep. The creatures peered out from their nests and dens, burrows and drays.

The sun was bright, but her power was weak. Wise and sensible mothers and fathers packed up their families and, buttoning vests and squashing caps over errant ears, marshalled their children into the caravans that were heading south to the warm steppes of the plains.

Those animals that slept the winter through checked their larders and made their final lists of provisions to collect from Nature's store: acorns and pinecones, the hard fruit of the sanddorn and chestnuts.

Not everyone left straightaway.

Those animals that had thick fur and long hair were not troubled by Jack.

They did, however, keep a lookout for Jill, who sprinkled the ground with snow and lit the crystal lamps that were hung from every twig."

Humblenot paused and looked up into the canopy above his head. The leaves parted and a sparrow dived down and settled on one of the finials that decorated the ends of the arms of the chair. The finials looked like skulls. The animals that had donated their braincases for the purpose of decorating Humblenot's chair could only be guessed at; some said 'griffin' and others, 'dragon mice'.

"Why do the birds gather and fly together in formation?" asked Humblenot.

Annick's hand shot up into the air.

"Answer wrong and you'll stay behind to wash the glasses."

Even though it wasn't possible to see Annick's face, it was obvious to all that the boy had swallowed very hard.

"The characteristic and easily recognised 'V' formation greatly increases the efficiency and range of the birds, especially over long distances. Each bird, except for the one at the front, benefits from the vortex of air created by the flapping of the wings of the bird ahead of it. This vortex helps each bird to support its own weight in flight. In a 'V' formation of twenty-five birds, each bird can achieve a reduction in wind resistance of up to sixty-five percent and as a result, increase its range by seventy-one percent. The birds flying at the ends of the formation and at the front are periodically rotated to spread flight fatigue equally among all the birds of the flock."

"Credit for your answer should go to Mistress Jane ... but I will allow you credit for remembering the answer verbatim."

"Do I still need to stay and wash the glasses?"

Humblenot roared with laughter and the trees shook so hard that a leaf and a nut fell into every child's lap. The Constable was transported back in time and remembered answering the same question. He alone had saved the leaf and the nut, whereas his friends had tossed them aside as they left the garden. The leaf had grown into a book of stories about the Dragon Lords and their wars with the Satyrs. The nut had swelled and cracked and when the Constable had opened the two halves, he had found a gold penny inside. The same penny still hung from his watch chain. The book was kept on the table beside his bed.

"*The birds began to leave the forest, saying a cheery*

goodbye to the creatures who were staying behind. Jack stayed awake longer each day and beat the hearth rugs in anticipation of the arrival of Jill. One by one the creatures that remained behind retreated into their burrows or dens to sleep the winter through. The last squadron of sparrows prepared to leave the forest.

A small boy, with a mean streak to him, was out of doors with his catapult, attempting to knock the last acorns from the ragged clusters that were hanging like varicose veins from the otherwise bare branches of the Duchess' oaks. He espied the squadron getting ready to leave. The first bird called order and all of the birds in the squadron flapped their wings to ready themselves for take-off. The flock rose and swooped to harry the Cream Maker's cat who was too fat to jump and catch them. They spiralled up like a swarm of locusts and made their formation.

The boy, whose name was Nicholas, took aim. Just as the sparrows were about to pass over the edge of the Festival Field, he let the catapult do its nasty work and the stone shot into the sky. Being the start of the journey, the sparrows were quick, all except for one who was suffering from a chill. The sparrow was already lagging behind. The stone clipped his wingtip, which caused him to tumble and, being weak, he couldn't right himself. He plummeted to the ground. Luckily for him, he landed in the vestiges of the hayrick. The boy, who'd had no great expectations of hitting anything, hadn't seen the bird fall. The bird was stunned and finding it hard to breathe. His little chest was already congested and had it not been for the Bull Dog, the little bird might have perished there and then."

"What is the name of the Bull Dog kept by the Blacksmith?"

Every child raised their hand.

"Too easy ... We all know her name is Cassandra. Keep your hand up if you know the names of the two dragons that watch my gate ..."

Slowly but steadily the hands fell as the children tried and failed to remember the names of the two dragons that watched the gate to the garden. The Constable realised his hand was still up and he blushed deeply.

"Constable! I should be ashamed of myself if I were the Constable and did not remember their names. Tell them wrong and you'll be washing the glasses!"

The children tittered into their hands.

"The names of the dragons that watch the gate to the storytelling garden are ... Igor and Eger ..."

Had he got it right?

"Clearly having a good memory is indispensable to the function of being the Constable. Be warned! Step into this garden without an invitation and the dragons will assume you are a thief and toast your backside to a cinder toffee and ... pull your legs off!"

Everyone shuddered.

"Be pleased to tell us, Humblenot; how did the Bull Dog save the little bird from perishing there and then?"

"What is your name, child?"

It was a needless question. Humblenot knew the names of all the children. He snipped the chord that attached them to their mummies, at the time of their birth. He used a pair of gold scissors that belonged to the Duchess. She hadn't found them in a hundred years, and it was a constant source of irritation to her.

"My name is Weave."

"You show a good deal of confidence for a girl of your age. I should be pleased to tell you the rest of the story."

"The Bull Dog saw the bird plummet out of the sky and land in the vestiges of the hayrick. Being a rotund sort of canine, he waddled over to the hayrick mess, convinced that the little bird would have broken its neck in the fall. It wasn't dead but it was very poorly. The Bull Dog, whose name was Rufus, picked up the little bird in his jaws and waddled back to the village with it. Bull Dogs are ill-equipped to administer first aid so he did the only thing he could think of. He took the bird to the forge and placed it very carefully near the forge pit where it was warm.

Content that the bird would come to no immediate harm, the Bull Dog went into the cottage to find a scrap of blanket in his basket. He returned to the side of the pit and covered the bird with the scrap.

"I can do no more; let God be merciful."

The bird was stunned and running a fever. Things did not look very promising."

"Now, remember that the time is just before Christmas and what do we expect to see just before Christmas?"

Again, every child's hand went up into the air.

"Jacob?"

"Holly with berries."

"Correct. Philly?"

"A Poinsettia displayed in the window of the Candle Maker's shop."

"Correct. Jonathan?"

"The stoat cloaked in his ermine robes."

"Correct. Michael?"

"Robin Red Breast."

"CORRECT!"

Humblenot clapped his hands together and a hundred dragonflies flew out of the mouths of the dragon guards at the gate and hovered in the garden, catching the stray beams of sunlight on their wings. Every child had a rainbow above their head and a copper penny fell out of their ears and onto their shoulders where it turned into a ladybird with thirteen spots. The ladybirds opened the little hard wing cases on their backs and took off, leaving a spot behind on the shoulder of each child. The spot grew into a toad, which croaked and hopped off to the Hammer Pond.

The children applauded the show.

"YES! Robin Red Breast visits us in the winter. Unlike most birds of his size, the Robin flies north not south. He is kept warm by a hot coal that he keeps in his heart."

"This day, one particular Robin arrived in the forest. He immediately went to the forge to share his fire with the Blacksmith's. Basking in the glow of the coals, the Robin fancied that he saw something move under a scrap of blanket that was resting on the ground by the pit. Robin was hungry having flown a very long way. Imagining that the scrap of cloth was perhaps

hiding a moth or a beetle, he fluttered down to the ground and picked up the corner of the blanket in his beak and pulled it back."

"You can imagine his surprise at finding the Sparrow."

"Sparrow! Whatever are you doing here? I left your bed made on the warm steppes of the southern plains."

The Sparrow was unable to answer. His little throat was parched.

"You do not look quite well. You have a foggy look in your eye and your tongue is bloated. I will endeavour to get you a drink of water."

The Robin, being accustomed with the forest, darted off to find an acorn cup. He found many and selected a strong one, clasping it firmly in his beak. He flew back over the Hammer Pond and skimmed the surface, filling the cup. Without spilling a drop, he returned to the sickbed of the Sparrow and very carefully poured a little water into the Sparrow's open beak. The Sparrow swallowed the precious fluid and coughed. Robin gave him some more water and soon the cup was empty.

"You cannot stay on the ground. The Cream Maker's cat will surely find you. I will away to find my bed, which I hope someone has made, and then I will return to bring you to safety."

"Thank you," croaked the Sparrow, already recovering quickly.

The Robin flew off, momentarily bathing in the warm up-draughts of the forge fire. He flew over the tops of young oaks and made his way to the Lock Keeper's cottage. The Lock Keeper's cottage, like all the rest, was thatched in hazel and willow. Under the eaves, he found a Swallow's nest, recently swept and newly made with the furry seed pods of Sheep Tuft.

"Thank you, Swallow. You will find your bed made in the bank of the creek that flows down to the plains."

Having found the nest and his bed made, the Robin flew back to the forge. The Sparrow was resting and no longer panting. His eyes had lost their fogginess and looked like two bright glass beads.

"Cousin; I have found my bed and you are welcome to share it. But I wonder if you can fly. Are you hungry?"

"*I had a worm yesterday. I am a little hungry. A morsel will give me the strength to make the journey if it is not too far.*"

"*The Lock Keeper's cottage.*"

"*Far enough.*"

"*Let me try and find a morsel; something sweet. The Confectioner's shop should be open and, being the giving season, it should be stocked with plenty of sweet things.*"

The Robin flew to the centre of the village, where the Square was being hung with coloured lanterns. In the middle of the Square, the Christmas tree was being erected and Timothy the Vitrine Maker was sorting the glass baubles that would be hung in the tree the following day. The Robin found the Confectioner's shop easily; the window was filled to bursting with gold foil-wrapped fondants. The light reflected off the surface of all those sweet wrappers and they looked like a thousand golden scarab beetles piled in the tomb of a Pharaoh.

"*I need a diversion. I suppose that must be the Cream Maker's cat I spy sitting under the Drover's bench. I've had plenty of practice in being chased by and alluding lions and cheetahs, so a fat cat shouldn't be too difficult to manage.*"

The Robin dived and, taking careful aim, he swooped in under the Drover's bench and pricked the behind of the cat, whose name was Marrakech. She was as fat as a barrel of cream. She had smoky grey fur and smudgy blue ears and rings around her eyes. Her tail was ringed like the Barber's pole. The Robin, having delivered the sting, hid in the Drover's cup, which was always hanging from the hook that had been fixed to the milepost which stood beside the trough. The cat let out a blood-curdling scream. The Confectioner heard the noise and came out of the shop to investigate the cause. They had very conveniently left the door open. Robin flew out of the cup, frightening the Confectioner, who had picked up the cat, who then promptly dropped her in the water trough.

With commotion in abundance erupting behind him, Robin flew into the shop and landed on the counter. Chocolates were no good because he couldn't pick them up in his little beak. In any event, he didn't think chocolate was all that good for birds. Then he espied the sugar sprinkled ginger cookies that were quite thin and crisp. The cookies offered a better prospect and he was able to pick one up by the edge, but only just. He took off and for a moment, sank alarmingly close to the floor, but his compassion fed his resolve to get the wafer to the Sparrow. He sped out of the door, frightening the Confectioner again, who dropped the cat into the rainwater butt.

"I believe it is the traditional time of year for a bath!" Robin sang out.

He delivered the wafer to the sick Sparrow, who pecked at the sweet golden biscuit greedily. The Robin was satisfied that his pluck had been appreciated by the Sparrow when the little bird could eat no more and some lustre had returned to Sparrow's feathers.

"Come! The cat will not forget the double dunking she had this afternoon, and while I have no fear that she is able to climb up to the eaves of the cottage, she will post guard at the door of the sweet shop from now on and our victuals may be a little harder to come by."

"I will try my hardest to make it all the way without stopping," promised Sparrow.

"I will carry what is left of the wafer. It'll be something for our tea!"

The sweet, sugary and spicy biscuit did the trick and Sparrow, with a good deal of encouragement from Robin, just made it to the Lock Keeper's cottage in one flight. Safely tucked up in the nest, the birds nibbled a little of the biscuit and put the rest away for later.

"I am worried, Sparrow. It is destined to get much colder and you have no jacket. If you've already had a chill, I shudder at the malady that may strike you down when Jill has arrived."

"What do you do in the winter, Robin? How do you survive?"

"I was forgetting that you are never here when it gets so cold that even the icicles have icicles. One winter, the Hammer Pond froze so hard that the villagers used it as a skating rink. The lock on the canal froze and the barge got stuck at Frew. The children's Christmas party food and decorations had to be carried to the village by the Duchess' carriage horses. A pretty sight they made."

Humblenot paused to drink another mouthful of the cordial

in his pail.

"Not that we see them very often, more's the pity, but the Duchess' carriage horses are born of a very noble line. Even if everyone in the County had a sovereign, there wouldn't be enough money to buy even one. How many carriage horses does the Duchess have?"

All the children knew the answer, "FOUR!" they sang out together.

The Duchess' carriage horses were as black as coal and their coats shone like volcanic glass. They wore plumes of ostrich and peacock feathers. Their bridles were fashioned from braided silver and gold and their saddles were made from the polished leathery hides of long-dead Dragons.

Humblenot returned to the story.

"How do you keep warm, Robin?" enquired Sparrow.

"I have a coal in my heart to keep me warm. It is why my chest is red. You don't have a coal and we dare not risk building a nest too close to the forge pit because the Cream Maker's cat will certainly look there first. You need a jacket to keep you warm."

"How did you get a coal in your heart?" enquired the Sparrow.

"Ah, now that's a story!" announced the Robin with a faraway look in his little beady eye. "Remind me to tell it to you on Christmas Day."

"How shall I get a jacket?"

"Angela, the Seamstress will have cloth and thread. We need to visit her worktable. On Christmas Eve, she will be at the service in the church and we might have just enough time to make you a jacket."

"That is the day after tomorrow," reported Sparrow confidently.

"Tomorrow, I must announce my arrival to the villager folk. I shall fly to the Square and sit on the milepost for all to see. My arrival is a reminder to all that the giving season is upon us and it is the time of year to be compassionate and generous."

"You've already saved my life!"

"I am duty-bound to honour the gift of the coal that sits in my breast and keeps me warm. You are welcome, Sparrow."

With the two of them in the nest, the birds were very cosy and soon fell asleep. With a warm bed and a tummy full of sweet biscuit, they had no trouble sleeping the whole night through. Not even the hoot from the Owl at three o'clock woke them up. The Owl always hooted at three o'clock in the morning to make sure that the Baker was awake and preparing the dough for the villagers' daily bread. In exchange for his alarm call, the Owl received the crumbs from the breadbasket.

CHAPTER FOUR

In the morning, Robin left Sparrow in bed and flew off to the Square to announce his arrival. He sat on the top of the milepost and puffed up his chest to display his red breast. Everyone who walked past smiled when they saw him. From his observation point, Robin was also able to keep a watch for Marrakech. He need not have worried. Marrakech had a frightful cold and was sneezing incessantly. The Cream Maker spoke to the Duchess, who called for the Veterinarian.

"Majesty, I suggest you send Marrakech to the coast of Africa. The warm winter sun will cure her of the cold. It was perhaps not wise to bathe her twice out of doors at this time of the year."

"The Confectioner dropped her, allegedly frightened by the Robin, who was attempting to raid the shop and steal biscuits. Whoever heard of such a thing? I have a good mind to send the Confectioner to Africa with Marrakech."

The Veterinarian thought that the Confectioner would not mind that too much.

"As your Majesty commands."

The Duchess was loathed to send Marrakech away. Even though the cat belonged to the Cream Maker, the Duchess thought of the cat as her own. Her own cat was scrawny and boss-eyed, and it displeased her to look upon the mog, who reminded the Duchess of her mother.

The sneezing became intolerable. The Duchess called for the Ambassador.

"Carry my darling Marrakech to the coast of Africa and place her in the care of the Sultan."

"As you command, Duchess. I will stay with her until she is properly better."

"Very good. You are dismissed."

The Ambassador was rather pleased with the commission. The cold aggravated his corns and bunions.

After the villagers had seen Robin, he flew back to the nest and shared a late breakfast with Sparrow.

"We must have of all stealth and cunning to get into the Seamstress' workshop. She has a cat if my memory serves me correctly," stated Robin.

"She does, Robin. The Ginger Tom."

"We will need to lure him out and keep him busy for an hour or two. I need to think, and this will require me to close my eyes for forty winks."

"What should I do, Robin?"

"We need a button for the jacket. If you have the strength and pluck, fly to the Garrison Room and look for a button on the floor. Bring it back."

The Sparrow was exceedingly happy to have been given this important job to do. He was also a little nervous. The soldiers in the Garrison Room were fearfully big and wore heavy boots. If he wasn't careful, he could very easily be squished flat. Reminding himself of just how brave Robin had been made him more confident.

"I can do this!"

Fortified by the last of the sweet wafer, he flew off to the Garrison Room. He sat by the chimney for a few minutes to warm his feet and his wingtips. The Sergeant Major opened the Garrison Room door and bellowed for the soldiers to come to attention and form their ranks on the Parade Ground. Twenty-five heavily shod soldiers trooped out and formed their ranks. Sparrow sneaked in through the window, which was open to cool the rice pudding that Cook had made. The floor of the Garrison Room was spotlessly clean as you might expect. There wasn't a speck of dust, let alone a button.

"Strength and pluck have brought me here. Now I have need of something else to find a button."

Just at that moment, Cook took off his jacket to have a rest from kneading the dough for the bread. The jacket was pristine white and was fastened with three gold buttons. Cook had hung it on the peg by the washbasin.

"If I can just peck through the thread ..."

While Cook was resting his eyes, Sparrow darted from the windowsill to the peg. Using his sharp little talons, he climbed down the jacket like an Alpine explorer, and began to peck at the thread of the first button. His tiny beak was hard-pressed to cut through the strong thread. Nevertheless, he persisted. Finally, he pecked through the last strand and ... the button fell onto the floor and rolled under one of the beds.

"Oh, that is such poor luck!" Sparrow exclaimed. "Dare I risk it with so many boots in such close proximity?"

He could hear the Sergeant Major putting the troops through their paces and judged that they would not be returning for a good long while. He dived under the bed and found the button. It was a good deal heavier, but not much bigger, than the wafer that Robin had carried from the Confectioner's.

"If I can get to the window sill, I can rest there for a moment."

He picked up the button by its edge and readied himself for the first stage of the journey. He hopped out from under the bed and took off. His timing could not have been more inopportune for the Cook woke up.

"Oy!" shouted the Cook.

The Sparrow dared not risk stopping and flew straight out of the window. Without a rest, he was soon flagging and dropping lower and lower and in danger of landing well short of the Lock Keeper's cottage.

It was obviously his lucky day because the Bull Dog came waddling along.

He landed on the Bull Dog's thick, strong back. The Bull Dog was so intent on snuffling for truffles that he didn't even notice Sparrow.

Fortunately for Sparrow, the Bull Dog went along the canal and passed the cottage. Having rested, Sparrow was able to carry the button up and into the nest.

"Well done, Sparrow! That is a fine button. I only hope my tailoring skills do it justice!"

"There's a fresh rice pudding on the window sill of the Garrison Room too."

"And not yet Christmas Day! Come on!"

The thick and creamy skin of the rice pudding, which was laced with nutmeg and cinnamon certainly compensated them for the effort and ensured that they had full bellies for the rest of the day.

"Do you have a plan to lure The Ginger Tom out of the workshop, Robin?"

"Yes! I was reminded of a story told by Humblenot in my youth about the wooden horse of Troy."

Humblenot paused and looked up. There was a faraway look in his eyes. The Constable had heard the story of the wooden horse of Troy and knew that the story was taken from ancient mythology. It couldn't be that Humblenot had actually witnessed the subterfuge of the Greeks and their sacking of the city. Could he?

"The proverb says that it is never wise to look a gift horse in the mouth. However, in the case of the Trojan Horse, circumspection may have been wiser! If something is too good to be true ... it usually is."

"If it pleases you, Humblenot; how did Robin and Sparrow lure The Ginger Tom out of the workshop?"

"Why are you always impatient to hear the end of the story, Maddie?"

"I'm frightened to walk through the forest when it gets dark."

"Have no fear for I, Humblenot, will carry you back to the edge of the forest."

Maddie wasn't entirely convinced that this would be a better thing. Nevertheless, she smiled sweetly.

"Robin; do we have a plan?"

"I believe we do, Sparrow. If this year is the same as all previous years, the Christmas Tree will be decorated tomorrow by the children. After they have decorated the tree, they have their

party at the Palace. Everyone who attends the party is given a present by the Duchess. The Seamstress will be given a plum pudding in a box like everyone else. Angela, the Seamstress will bring the box back to the workshop after the party but before the church service. We'll hide in the box and let Angela carry us into the workshop."

"What of the cat?"

"This is where we get sneaky! The children always hang sugar mice in the tree. We will need to carry one of them to the workshop and place it on the lid of the copper and make sure that the cat sees it. Once Angela has left for the church, the cat will spring on the mouse and the lid will give way under his weight and he will plunge into the copper."

"Will he not jump back out?"

"It is very deep. I have no doubt that he will try to jump back out, but I have every faith in Newton's Law. And don't forget, the mouse will fall in too. Perchance the cat thinks it is Christmas Day already if he finds himself in a barrel with a mouse!"

"That is a sneaky plan, Robin. What should I have done had you not arrived back?"

"We do not need to worry about that. Right! I am tired from our various exertions, and thinking up a plan as sneaky as this has been especially tiring. We'll go to our bed and wake up bright and early and do a bit of scouting. We have two very dangerous tasks to accomplish in a relatively short space of time."

"I'm so happy you are my friend, Robin. Goodnight!"

"Goodnight, Sparrow. God bless you and grant you happy dreams."

CHAPTER FIVE

Both slept very soundly as a result of the delicious rice pudding skin that filled their bellies, and neither of them heard the Owl's hoot at three o'clock. The Baker was already awake, making the Christmas loaves.

Just as Robin had feared, Jill came a-sprinkling through the village that night. Sparrow's shivers woke them both up.

"Jill's arrived!"

"That is why my toes are numb."

"Let us be off to the forge pit to warm our extremities and be the first to grab the Baker's burnt offering."

Humblenot stopped to pose a question.

"How many loaves are there in a Baker's dozen?" he asked.

Maddie was the first to raise her hand.

"Be warned! A wrong answer will cost you a farthing for every tuppence in your tin."

"If it pleases you to know the answer, Humblenot, it is thirteen."

"And why is it thirteen and not twelve?"

"Allowance is made just in case the Baker burns one."

"It appears I shall have to look for my farthings somewhere else!"

Maddie was mightily pleased with herself to have saved the farthings' forfeit. Though, being the Baker's daughter, she did have the advantage over the others!

"Robin and Sparrow flew hurriedly to the forge pit and warmed their wingtips. Nobody else had ventured out of doors just yet. The appearance of Jill had made everyone a little tardy in starting their day's labours. The Baker alone was working and just at that moment, he was taking the loaves out of the oven.

"Get ready, Sparrow. I smell a burnt crust and that is a good thing for us!"

Sure enough, the Baker had let one of the loaves burn. While it was still hot, he broke the cob up into small pieces and cast them out into the swept yard of the Bakery. Robin and Sparrow dived onto the crumbs with gusto. The Baker stood and watched the birds at their feasting for a few minutes.

The tinkle of the doorbell in the shop called him away. It was Old Mother Eve come to collect the baps for the party.

Thus, heated on the outside by the forge pit and on the inside by the warm crumbs, the two little birds flew off to the church to listen to the choir practise for the carol service. Once the Pastor was satisfied with the cadence, they quit the church and nestled under the eaves of Timothy's shop and waited for the children to begin to decorate the tree.

"The sugar mouse will be quite heavy, Robin. Do you think we can manage it?"

"Between us, I have every confidence., Sparrow."

They watched and waited. The children, dressed in their winter coats and boots, assembled outside Timothy's shop. He brought forth the decorations and they trooped off together to decorate the tree.

The Confectioner delivered the white and pink sugar mice. The Magistrate found the star for the top of the tree. The tree was quite tall, so the Blacksmith brought the ladder and the Constable climbed to the top of the tree and fixed the star in its place. He also had to hang some of the decorations in the upper branches. In so doing, he knocked a good quantity of snow off the boughs onto the heads of the children below.

This resulted in a general call to arms and the first snowball fight of the season got underway. Pretty soon, everyone was wet, albeit flushed and laughing.

The boys dried off at the forge pit and the girls dried off at the Baker's bread oven.

Once the lanterns had been lit, the children assembled with the Guard and they were led by the Sergeant Major to the Palace for the party with the Duchess.

"Now for the first part of the plan, Sparrow."

The birds fluttered down and found a sheltered spot on a

lower bough from which to survey the prospects for success.

"How will we carry it, Robin?"

"They are hung from the branches by a ribbon. If we poke our heads through from the back and take off precisely at the same time, we might just be able to slip the ribbon off the branch, and while the ribbon is around our necks, we can carry it between us."

"We will be very close to each other, Robin. I fear our wings will get in each other's way."

"I have an idea. I will be on your right and you will be on my left. I will place my left wing on your back, and you will place your right wing on mine. Then we shall only have to flap one wing each."

"If we move to the end of this branch, there is a mouse hanging from the branch above it, which is directly in front of us."

They tiptoed forward and found they could just reach. They popped their heads through the loop of the ribbon and placed a wing on each other's back.

"After three, Sparrow ... Are you ready?"

"I'm ready. Can I just confirm that we are flying with this mouse to the back of the Seamstress' workshop where we will place the mouse on the edge of the lid of the copper so that the cat can see it?"

"Exactly right! Okay; after three ... one ... two ... three!"

They flapped their one wing in time together with help from Robin, who could count. They shot forward and, with a bit of a tug, they lifted the ribbon and slipped it off the branch.

The weight of the mouse was roughly the same as half the weight of a small bird. Thus, they each had a quarter of their own weight to carry.

"We're going to do it!" chirped Sparrow.

"... one ... two ... one ... two ... one ... two," Robin continued to call out to make sure that they beat their wings in time together.

They made a good height and then glided down to the copper behind the Seamstress' workshop where they landed on the lid in a bit of an untidy heap.

37

They slipped the ribbon from around their necks and Robin, being a little bit stronger, nudged the mouse so that its head was just peeping over the edge of the lid.

"Now we wait until the Seamstress leaves the party with her present."

"Are you confident that you can make me a jacket, Robin?"

"I have never made one before but I am confident of making a reasonable attempt."

"Oh dear! We forgot the button!"

"Then we shall have to take a needle and cotton with us and sew it on once we are back in the nest."

"We are both skilled at weaving nests. I am sure we can manage to sew on a button between us," Sparrow proclaimed.

"I am sure we can."

The children's party lasted for two hours. During which time, the birds feasted on the gingerbread crumbs that the Baker had left on the bird table before they flew up to the Palace to watch the children at their party games.

When the children assembled to leave for the walk back to the village for the church service, Robin and Sparrow flew into the lofty banqueting hall. They slipped into the box that contained the plum pudding that Angela the Seamstress had been given by the Duchess.

She carried the box back home by the ribbon with which it was secured. The birds were squished between the sides of the box and the rich plum pudding.

"I've had worse rides in my time," said Robin, a little intoxicated from the fumes of the brandy that the plums had been soaked in.

The Seamstress returned home and shortly afterwards; she heard the church bell that announced that the service would begin in fifteen minutes. She placed the box on the table.

Before she left, she put the cat out in the yard, fearing that the aroma of brandy-rich plums and spices would be too much for Ginger Tom to resist.

She needn't have worried. The Ginger Tom spied the mouse and jumped up onto the lid of the copper, which could not bear his weight. The cat, the mouse and the lid ended up at the bottom of the copper.

The birds waited for the Seamstress to leave for the church and then pecked their way out of the box.

"What colour jacket do you wish to have, Sparrow?" asked Robin, confronted by piles of fabric in every colour of the rainbow.

"A red one like yours, please!"

They found some bright red material on the workbench that the Seamstress had been working with to make a new cape for Maddie. Robin dragged a remnant out of the work pile with his beak.

"This will do handsomely! Now we need some thread."

"Here is some gold thread, Robin. Unless you think it will look too smart."

"Nonsense! Gold thread and a gold button!"

Using the Seamstress' own measuring tape, Robin took some vital measurements and began to peck out the shape of the jacket from the red fabric.

In fact, it wasn't so much a jacket as a waistcoat.

"It'll be easier to flap your wings, Sparrow if the jacket doesn't have arms."

"Agreed!"

Once Robin had marked out the basic shape, they were both able to peck and save considerable time.

It was thirsty work. Fortunately, the Seamstress had left a glass of elderberry cordial on the table from which they refreshed themselves.

"Nearly done!" announced Robin.

Once they had pecked out the shape and the hole through which Sparrow would pop his head, he tried it on.

"Now I just have to sew up the sides a little way to keep it from flying off.

"It will look like one of the tabards that the crusader Knights wore over their chain mail," announced Sparrow.

"The button will close the throat up tight to stop chills, and I'd say you'll look more like the Bishop than the Bishop himself!"

They threaded the needle. Sparrow held the needle in his beak and Robin passed the thread through the eye.

"Easier than a worm; the thread doesn't wriggle!"

Once the needle was threaded, Robin very carefully sewed up the sides of the tabard. He was very skilled, as are all birds, in weaving and sewing nests together.

Humblenot paused again. Uncharacteristically, he left the chair and went into the deep recess of the dwelling. There was absolute hush in the garden because no-one knew what Humblenot was going to do, not even the Constable.

But then the Constable smiled and a few moments later, Humblenot returned wearing his tabard.

"Why does a Knight wear a tabard over his chain mail?"

The children universally scratched their heads. Eventually, Mistress Jane held up her hand.

"Ah! Mistress Jane."

"On the battlefield, Knights of the one side would be differentiated from the Knights of the opposing side. This would prevent Knights on the same side from mistaking each other as the enemy."

"Quite right ... but ... it isn't always easy to see your enemy. He may wear the same tabard as you but harbour ill thoughts just the same. Wearing a tabard of one colour or another does not mark you out as a good person or a bad person; that mark is to be found upon your heart."

"But Humblenot, if it pleases you to be questioned, how can we see the mark on a person's heart? It's inside their body."

"That is a very good question, Jemaah. How can we tell if someone has a good heart?"

"By their acts of kindness?"

"Yes, Jacob ... and?"

"By their love for their family and friends?"

"Yes, Sally ... and for their neighbours ... and ...?"

"By their respect for Mother Nature and all of the animals?"

"Yes, Pru' ... and their respect for the Law and Reason."

Humblenot nodded in the direction of the Constable.

"The Robin secured the end of the thread with a knot and bit through the yarn, "There!"

Sparrow caught his reflection in the Seamstress' looking glass.

"Gracious, Robin. I have a red breast just like yours!"

"Yes you do, and for the duration of the winter, you will be a Robin to all intents and purposes."

The birds left the worktable and flew back out through the fanlight above the front door. They peered into the copper to check on the cat. He was licking the sugar mouse and seemed very content. He looked up and saw what he thought was two Robins.

"Peek ..."

"... a boo!"

He never hunted for birds again.

The Robin had secured the needle and some thread into the hem of the tabard so that they could sew on the button once they had returned to the nest. Sparrow held the button in place and Robin sewed it on. Then he did the button up and secured the neck of the tabard snug against the throat of the Sparrow.

"There; we've done it!"

"Robin, how can I ever thank you?"

"Sparrow, it is my duty to help you and honour the gift of the coal in my heart. You are very welcome."

"Will you tell me the story of how you received the coal in your heart?"

"I will tell you tomorrow. It is Christmas Day and the day for gifts. The story will be my gift to you."

"But I don't have a gift for you, Robin."

"Companionship, Sparrow; that is your gift to me. I would also be very surprised if there are not occasions during the winter when I shall have need of your help."

"You would not even have to ask, Robin."

They celebrated their enterprise and friendship by flying back to the village to listen to the songs being sung around the tree. Many a warm crumb found its way into their bellies too!

"Goodnight, Robin."

"Goodnight, Sparrow."

CHAPTER SIX

When they woke up on Christmas Day, there was not a sound to be heard.

"It is so quiet, Robin."

"I believe Jill has been sweeping out the corners of the mountains."

They peeked out and saw the snow lying thick and even.

"It is Christmas Day!"

"It is Christmas Day!"

The birds were snug enough in their nest. Robin had his coal and Sparrow had his jacket. They both had full bellies!

"I do not believe I could fly even if I had to," exclaimed Robin.

"Not even for mincemeat tart?"

"Ah; for that I might make the effort!"

"The Duchess has mincemeat tart today," Sparrow reminded him.

"It's a long way to the Palace. However, I would spend the energy just to see the face of the Bishop when he sees you!"

"I would rather hear the story of how you got the coal," admitted Sparrow.

"Well; the story takes place a very long time ago, in the country we know as Nepal. In those times, Robins did not have coals in their hearts, and they felt the cold of the winter as all birds did.

In order to keep warm, Cousin Robin perched on the roof of the monastery. The fire in the hearth was lit day and night to keep the Monks and the Nuns warm as they chanted their mantras."

"What is a mantra?"

"A kind of prayer. That winter, it was particularly cold, and the Rinpoche fell ill. He was very, very old. A young Monk sat beside his master's bed and prayed very hard for the dear old Rinpoche to get better."

"What is a Rinpoche?"

"He is the head of the monastery and he is very wise. The young Monk asked the Rinpoche what he could do to aid the Rinpoche's recovery. The Rinpoche replied that some medicine might help. The young Monk looked for the medicine everywhere, but he couldn't find any.

He returned to the side of his master's bed and relayed the bad news. The Rinpoche remembered that the medicine was made by an old woman who lived in a village that was one day's walk from the monastery.

The young Monk promised the old Rinpoche that he would walk to the village and fetch the medicine.

The snow was lying thick on the ground but despite having no yak and no boots, the young Monk set out early the next day to walk to the village."

"What is a yak?"

"A kind of cow. The young Monk clasped the folds of his robes to his throat and marched on, insensible to the numbing cold."

"How did he ignore the cold?"

"He chanted a mantra, a special prayer which served to remind him of his oath to feel compassion for his fellow man and to do whatever was necessary to ease their suffering."

"Do you know this mantra?"

"All Robins know it. It is 'Om Ma Ni Ped Me Hung Hri'..."

"I shall learn it myself!"

"The young Monk soldiered on and eventually found the village just before sunset.

He was welcomed and given a seat by the fire, where a bowl of steaming potato stew was placed in his hands.

He asked for some medicine for the Rinpoche. The old woman came forth with a stoppered phial that contained some of the medicine.

With many prayers of thanks, the young Monk went to bed

with a lighter heart, knowing he simply had to walk back the way he'd come."

"His toes must have been perishing cold!"

"They were, Sparrow, but his compassion allowed him to put aside his own discomfort. In the morning, the young Monk left the village.

The sky was threatening black and the clouds were scurrying across the sky like scolded cats. The wind increased and it began to snow heavily.

Very soon, the tracks he had left the day before were hidden and he realised that he was lost."

"Oh no!"

"Fear not, Sparrow. Being a curious bird, Cousin Robin had followed him to the village. Cousin Robin didn't need tracks in the snow to find his way back.

He fluttered mid-air in front of the young Monk and chirped the mantra. He then flew a little way ahead.

The young Monk realised that the little bird was guiding him back. He followed Cousin Robin and joined him in chanting the mantra.

By sunset, he saw the top of the dome of the monastery's stupa."

"What is a stupa?"

"A sacred building. A stupa contains all the mantras known to the Monks and sacred objects that transmit energy to all of mankind. The young Monk was overjoyed and quickened his steps to reach the monastery before the last rays of the sun disappeared. Even before he had warmed himself, he delivered the precious medicine to the Rinpoche, who by now was suffering a terrible fever. All of the Monks and Nuns prayed for the Rinpoche's recovery. In the morning, the Rinpoche was much recovered and asked his nurse to bring the young Monk to his bedside. The young Monk came quickly. The Rinpoche expressed his thanks as deeply as he knew how to. The young Monk received the Rinpoche's thanks graciously and turned to leave. Before the young Monk left, the Rinpoche asked him about the storm. The young Monk recounted how the little bird had guided him back.

"You acted selflessly to fetch me the medicine. The little bird acted selflessly to guide you back home, delivering us both. Such actions cannot go overlooked. Ask the bird what he would have in return."

The young Monk found the bird perched on the temple roof, warming his feet and wingtips. He asked the bird what he would have in return for his compassion and bravery. The little bird said that their thanks and prayers were enough. The young Monk reported back. The Rinpoche sat up in his bed and thought about the little bird a great deal. The Rinpoche ordered a 'fire puja' for the following day."

"What is a puja?"

"It is a special ceremony, Sparrow. The following day a fire was lit in the monastery courtyard and offerings were made. Mantras were sung and the Rinpoche himself was able to attend for a short time. The young Monk pointed out the little bird to the old man. Cousin Robin was sitting on the roof of the temple as usual. The Rinpoche held out his hand and beckoned for the little bird to come down. Cousin Robin fluttered down and settled in the palm of the old man's hand. The Rinpoche expressed his thanks for the guidance that the little bird had given to the young Monk. The Rinpoche asked the bird if he liked the fire puja. Cousin Robin told him that he liked the puja very much, especially in the wintertime! It gave the Rinpoche an idea.

At the end of the ceremony, when the embers of the fire were hot and glowing bright red, the Rinpoche picked out a small one and put it inside a little silver locket. He hung the locket around the neck of the little bird. The ember warmed the silver box and the heat radiated out and kept the little bird warm, even in the harshest weather. In the spring, Cousin Robin found a mate. It was still quite cold, and Cousin Robin shared the warmth of the ember in the silver locket with his Darling Rosita. They raised a family of three chicks. Cousin Robin and Darling Rosita were overjoyed, but they worried that there would not be enough heat for them all come the wintertime. In the spring, when the chicks were born, their plumage was speckled and brown. As the spring changed to summer and the summer changed to autumn, the chicks fledged and gained their adult feathers. No more astounding a sight had Cousin Robin and Darling Rosita seen; the chicks had bright red breasts!

Cousin Robin visited the Rinpoche and questioned him.

"Cousin Robin, the warmth of compassion will live in the hearts of Robins forevermore. A Robin will never feel cold."

Cousin Robin went back to his Darling Rosita and the babies. He recounted what the Rinpoche had said.

"We must honour this gift," they all agreed.

Sparrow had tears in his eyes by the time Robin had finished recounting the tale.

"That is a beautiful story, Robin."

"And every word is true. I have a coal in my heart and I never feel cold!"

"And you have honoured the gift."

"Even in the trying alone, the fire is fed and the coal glows red."

Humblenot wiped his own tears away with the back of his hand.

"That is the story of the Robin and the Sparrow and this is the reason why the Robin has a red breast."

All of the children shed a tear. The tears ran down their cheeks and fell onto the ground. There they grew into Dew Bugs that scuttled off. Each bug carried a pail that held the precious tear, and with it, they watered the thirsty young oak saplings.

The Constable withdrew his white handkerchief and blew his nose very hard. Mistress Jane withdrew her dainty lilac handkerchief and dabbed at the corners of her eyes.

"Now, all of my questions were answered correctly. How then will the glasses be washed and dried ready for the next storytelling?" queried Humblenot.

The children got up from their toadstools and all washed their own glass, drying them on Dock leaves and placing them back on the two trays. Clara and Hugo put the glasses away in the cupboard, and Mistress Jane clapped her hands to gain everyone's attention.

"Children; I hope you enjoyed the story as much I did. If we can all try to be a little bit more like the Robin, then the world will be a happier, kinder place. Now, we need to thank Humblenot for the story and make our way back to the village before sunset."

"THANK YOU, HUMBLENOT!" sang out thirty young voices.

"Thank you for listening. Respect the forest and the creatures that dwell here. Now! I promised Maddie a ride back as far as the young oaks."

With Maddie perched on his shoulder, Humblenot led the children back through the forest. At the Witches' Willow, they all whistled the Duchess' Birthday Song. The Constable was bringing up the rear, trying very hard to quell his fear and the memory of the day when Henrietta had let go of his hand and abandoned him.

Today, he needn't have worried so much. Henrietta was waiting by the tree and held his hand all the way back to the village.

The End

(ps. Look out for the next story –
Humblenot & The Rat & The Cat)

Printed in Great Britain
by Amazon